A Straw
for Two

A Straw for Two

story by ÉRIC SANVOISIN
illustrations by MARTIN MATJE

UNE PAILLE POUR DEUX
translated by GEORGES MOROZ

Delacorte Press

Published by
Delacorte Press
a division of
Random House, Inc.
1540 Broadway
New York, New York 10036

First American Edition 1999
First published by Les Éditions Nathan, Paris, 1998

Text copyright © 1998 by Éric Sanvoisin
Illustrations copyright © 1998 by Martin Matje
Translation copyright © 1999 by Georges Moroz

Library of Congress Cataloging-in-Publication Data
Cataloging-in-Publication Data is available from the Library of Congress.
ISBN: 0-385-32702-1
The text of this book is set in 15-point Goudy.
Manufactured in the United States of America
October 1999
10 9 8 7 6 5 4 3 2
PHO

For Janine and Bernard . . .

A Straw
for Two

one

The Lonely Young Ink Drinker

Ever since my encounter with Draculink, the ink-drinking vampire, I've been drinking books like crazy. How, you ask? With a straw, of course!

Chapter after chapter I suck in the stories. They're absolutely delicious! As soon as the ink from the books makes its way into my mouth, I feel a tickle on the tip of my tongue. Instantly I get a taste of all kinds of adventures. Sometimes I'm a pirate on a proud three-masted ship. Sometimes I'm an astronaut rocketing into space. Sometimes I'm an ordinary human being. Sometimes I'm a cat.

With my straw, I live a thousand lives. Each of them different. Each of them thrilling. The  only problem is that no one must know. So I consume the books in secret, sucking the ink and swallowing the words when no one is watching. It goes without saying that I do this at night. That's the easy part.

The hard part is that I can't share my straw with anyone. I'm very lonely.

Dad owns a bookstore. He'd pass out if he knew about my taste for the ink in books. You see, once I use my straw, the books' pages are totally blank. The books become unreadable. Unsellable. Good for the garbage. Good for the fireplace.

Sometimes I tackle the faded pages of the old books at the public library. I also "recycle" the books people get rid of because they take up too much space. But I don't dare handle what Dad calls his "little bookies." He's too crazy about them, and anyway, his customers would complain and he'd start asking himself questions. . . .

I get chills when I think that he might someday discover my secret. My entire family would be afraid of me and probably stay far away. I don't

want to end up living in a cemetery, an old and lonely ink drinker like Draculink.

Draculink is ancient. He used to be a bloodthirsty vampire. But one day he got a bad case of indigestion. Too much blood, I guess. Ever since, he's been an ink drinker. He still sleeps in a coffin like other vampires, but he can go out in the daylight. That's how he came to bite me: he visited the bookstore in the middle of the afternoon. I didn't suspect his identity, but something about him made me follow him out of the store. That's how he came to write his vampire name on my arm with his teeth: *Draculink.*

We haven't seen each other since that day. He looks really bizarre and gives me the chills. Still, I've decided to go to the cemetery tonight to ask him an important question:

"Mr. Draculink, can I bite a girl so that she becomes like me?"

So that I can share my secret and not be lonely anymore. Well, I won't go into all these details, which are none of his business. I worry about his answer. If he says no, that means I'll remain alone for a lifetime. . . .

two

Death on My Heels

I waited until my parents went to bed; then I tiptoed out of the house. Since I began drinking ink, I have become light as a feather and can move as silently as a pair of slippers.

It was dark outside. But I have the eyes of a cat, courtesy of all the books about cats that I've drunk. So nighttime is luminous for me. It's as though the stars were lighting up the sky like thousands of flashlights.

Straight to the cemetery I went, with my teeth clenched. What a crazy place it is. By day, the gravestones are just monuments decorated with religious symbols and flowers. At

night, they squeak and turn into frightening shadows. I said to myself, "You're an ink drinker. No harm can come to you." But I didn't believe a word.

Gingerly I went down the stairs of Draculink's monument. The steps were very slippery. At the bottom I knocked on the wall, since there was no door. I didn't want to enter without warning. I had done that once—on the memorable day when everything started—and Draculink got angry.

No answer.

"Anybody here?" I whispered.

Odd. None of the candles in the vaulted monument was lit; the first time, several of them had been burning. Stepping forward like a blind person, I stretched out my arms in front of me. Maybe Draculink was taking a walk or sleeping soundly.

Just in case, I had brought a small flashlight with me. I turned it on. The ink drinker's casket was still in the same spot, but it was empty. At the back of the

room, his pantry was filled with books. But something wasn't right. After taking a few more steps, I caught sight of a second casket near the first one. Lower and smaller, the casket looked just my size.

A frightening thought chilled me to the bone. Draculink wanted to adopt me! Since he was one of the living dead, he was going to kill me so that I would live in the vaulted grave with him. But I didn't want to leave my parents! I just wanted to remain a boy who happened to be an ink drinker.

Horrified, I backed up abruptly. My arm hit the big casket, which slid from its pedestal, then teetered for a moment on the edge before tipping over and crashing to the floor.

I was petrified. Draculink would never forgive me for wrecking his old wooden box.

Not waiting for his return, I rushed out of the vault faster than a speeding bullet. I was imagining Draculink's presence all around me. Death was on my heels!

three

Carmilla

The next day at school, I was definitely not in great shape. I sat alone at my desk at the back of the classroom, feeling lonelier than ever. There was no way I could reveal my horrifying secret to my friends without instantly becoming a monster in their eyes.

No one could possibly understand me—no one, that is, but another ink drinker my age. . . .

A little casket was grinning in my head. It seemed to be saying, "I'll get you anyway! There's no escape!" No wonder I was hardly paying attention to what the teacher, Ms. Muzard, was saying.

"Odilon! Move your backpack so that Carmilla can sit next to you."

"Huh? What?"

I had totally forgotten about the new student arriving that day. It was a girl, and I had to be the one to share my desk with her. Bad news! My heart was as dark and cold as a crypt, and I was not in a sharing mood. Grumbling, I made space for Carmilla, who

quietly sat next to me. I glanced over at her, just to see what she looked like. She smiled.

Suddenly I completely forgot about Draculink, about the little casket that was destined for me, and about the large wrecked casket.

Carmilla was prettier than the prettiest girl in school. Her smile was like sunshine. I touched my forehead. Burning hot! I stopped listening to Ms. Muzard. The assignment was to draw a map of our country, with the capital and the main cities. I drew a heart instead, with a capital named Carmilla.

At recess, I didn't get a chance to talk to Carmilla, but I kept my eyes on her at all times. Something drew me to her like a magnet.

The problem was that I was not the only Prince Charming in the running. Jonathan flirted with her, and Max couldn't stop making goo-goo eyes at her. Meanwhile, I did nothing. I was paralyzed.

Then I thought about Draculink again and the question I wanted to ask him about girls. Could one of them become like me?

I decided to bite Carmilla, just to see. . . .

four

What Would You Do if I Bit You?

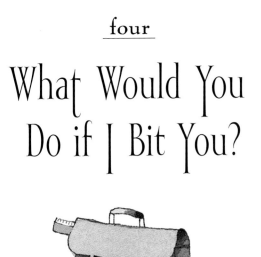

The next day, as I was about to copy the assignments Ms. Muzard had written on the blackboard, panic struck!

In my backpack, I found that my notebook had been almost entirely "drunk." All the homework I'd done for Monday, Tuesday,

19

Wednesday, Thursday and Friday had vanished. Was it a warning from Draculink? He had no doubt tracked me down and would soon show up at school! My thoughts switched from Carmilla to ways I might escape from the old ink drinker. I could not think of any. Unless I moved very far from here—but convincing my parents to move would be next to impossible. . . .

"You're as white as a ghost. Something wrong?"

It was the first time Carmilla had spoken to me. My ears became red. I made a superhuman effort to smile at her. All things considered, I still had a chance. Jonathan and Max were out of the race. Carmilla didn't want them.

"I have a crush," I said.

"Ah! Then it's nothing to worry about. It's a nice illness. No need for a cure."

She didn't even ask me who I had a crush on. Maybe she didn't care. So I played my last card. No room for a mistake.

"What would you do if I kissed you?" I asked.

I was actually thinking, "What would you do if I bit you?" Unfortunately, the three o'clock bell started ringing. Carmilla gathered her things and shot to the exit like a rocket. What about the answer to my question?

I ran after her. She had no right to drop me like that! As I passed Jonathan and Max, I slowed down. I didn't want them to guess what was going on. But from the way I was blushing, they understood that I too was faring poorly. I heard them laughing behind my back.

In the street I spotted Carmilla's coat. She was turning the corner near an apartment building. I had to move as fast as a lightning bolt to catch her. If I didn't, I'd be spending a dreary weekend waiting for Monday to arrive.

I sprinted and caught up a little, but Carmilla was running like Cinderella at the ball when the clock struck midnight. Where was she going? At the rate she was moving, she'd soon be out of town.

Before I could catch up, she disappeared into the cemetery. I ran after her through the gates. A shiver shot up and down my entire body. Draculink was somewhere around. . . .

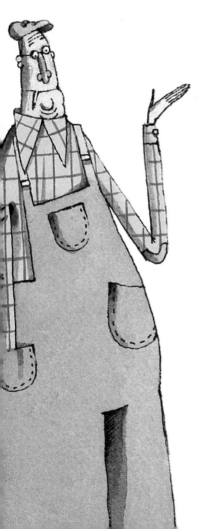

I decided that Carmilla was probably the daughter of the cemetery groundskeeper. Why else would she have raced over here? I found my courage and rang the bell at the groundskeeper's house. The place looked old and dilapidated. A disheveled man opened the door. A threadbare cap covered his head, and he was hunched over.

"What do you want?" he asked.

"Sir, I would like to see Carmilla. She left something at school!"

"Carmilla? Who's that?"

I realized that Carmilla did not live here. So what was she doing in this gloomy place?

"Wait a minute. Carmilla, Carmilla . . . It rings a bell. I must figure this out."

The groundskeeper put on his coat, grabbed a flashlight and slammed the door on his way out. I saw the roof vibrate and took a step backward. A tile fell two inches away from me.

"Nothing to worry about. Repairs are over-due, but who's got time for that? Follow me."

The sky was getting dark. . . . My guide moved in and out of the pathways the way I do in my neighborhood streets. He knew everyone there. He was constantly saying "Good evening, madam," "Good evening, sir." And more than once I thought I heard sounds like sighs answering him. From behind, he looked like Quasimodo. One shoulder was much higher than the other, and his gait reminded me of a chimpanzee. How could he possibly have been Carmilla's father? It was nighttime now. I wished I had not followed him.

Eventually he stopped in front of a very old and beautiful grave. I knew it well, since it was there, when we first met, that Draculink had passed on to me his taste for ink.

"It's here. Carmilla, Carmilla, what an odd first name."

Before I could say a word, the grounds-keeper turned and limped off. At the end of the pathway, he vanished into the darkness.

I turned toward the ink bottle–shaped grave and found myself face to face with a freshly painted mailbox. A label was glued on it:

Miss Carmilla
c/o Mr. Draculink

five

The Blue Taste of Southern Seas Ink

I was dumbstruck!

If Carmilla lived here, it meant she was a . . . No! It was too unbelievable. But it made sense . . . she was the one who had drunk my notebook! This also meant that the little casket in the crypt was hers.

All of a sudden, I felt a presence behind me. An uncanny presence . . .

A smell of old paper and ink dust wafted from the creature.

"Go downstairs," he ordered in a raspy voice. "Carmilla is waiting for you."

It was Draculink.

"I . . . I apologize for what happened with the casket. It was an accident."

"Downstairs!"

With my legs shaking, I headed down into the crypt. He stayed outside. No possible exit.

Downstairs, all the candles were lit. Carmilla was sitting in the little casket, waiting for me. Nearby, the big casket had been repaired with planks and nails. Carmilla looked at me intently. I did not know to what to say.

"Want a drink?"

She pointed at the books in the pantry. I shook my head. My throat felt tight.

"Do you remember the question you asked me this afternoon?"

No. I had no recollection whatsoever. I was feeling like a fly in a spider's web. I felt hot. I felt cold. Outside, Draculink was keeping a silent watch.

Carmilla's eyes, like two shining moons, were staring at me. Once more I felt hot. Once more I felt cold.

"You wanted to kiss me. Well, you may!"

She closed her moonlike eyes. I moved nearer to the small casket. The flames of the candles danced in the breeze and cast a porcelain glow on her cheeks. My legs were like lead. I couldn't put one foot in front of the other.

Carmilla looked like a doll.

Meanwhile, upstairs, Draculink was waiting.

My lips almost touched Carmilla's cheek. She smelled like an orange blossom. I said to myself, "Carmilla is a cake I am about to taste." But she stopped me.

"No, not like that. Do you really like me or not?"

I blushed. I was embarrassed and hesitated again about what to do next. After all, Draculink was keeping watch upstairs. And Carmilla had woven her web to catch me.

I kissed her. Total dizziness. Her lips tasted like the blue ink from the southern seas. Then she bit me so as to imprint her name into my skin.

I looked at my arm in disbelief. Not so long ago, Draculink had bitten me in the very same spot to make an ink drinker out of me. His name had remained embedded in my skin like a tattoo. Now it was getting blurred while, gradually, Carmilla's name became clearer and clearer.

"Why did you do that, Carmilla?"

"So everyone will know that you really, really like me!"

Then Draculink showed up. He yawned, lay down and fell asleep at once. Carmilla moved the blanket up to his chin so that he would not be cold.

"He is my uncle," she revealed. "I am living in his home."

I didn't sleep near Carmilla that night. Her casket was too narrow and the crypt too chilly. Anyway, my parents would have been worried sick about my absence.

As I hurried through town in the dark, the memory of Carmilla's lips illuminated the way.

Later, in my bed, I dreamed that this was not a dream.

DRACMILLA
CARMILLVRE

six

Breakfast for Two with One Straw

The next day, Carmilla and I ate breakfast together. She had invented a straw with two ends so that we could drink the same book simultaneously.

When she swallowed the beginning of a sentence, I relished the end. When she ran through fields with bison, I felt out of breath. When she fell, I stood up. And when the hero kissed the love of his life, I could taste Carmilla's lips on my own. We were starting page forty when—

"Hum, hum . . ."

It was Draculink. He grumbled as he got out of his oddly repaired casket and gave us a look of disapproval. One straw for two was not his preference. He was obviously an old, selfish vampire.

"Where are you going, Uncle?" Carmilla asked between two sips of adventure.

Without turning his head, he bellowed:

"I'm going to fetch a little casket for your little friend. This way, should he decide to become a normal ink drinker, he will be able to stay and sleep here. To sleep in a bed, under the roof of a modern house, with central heating and water—why, the very thought of it is horrifying and gives me goose bumps!"

He left.

Then Carmilla told me:

"You know, whether I sleep in a casket or in a bed doesn't make any difference."

I sighed with joy. And then I started another book, titled *The Ink Drinker*. . . .

It was a most wonderful and tasty book!

About the Author

ÉRIC SANVOISIN is one bizarre writer. Using a straw, he loves to suck the ink from all the fan letters he receives. That's what inspired him to write this story. He's sure that just as there are blood brothers and blood sisters, everyone who reads this book will become his ink brother or ink sister. If you write to him, he will send you a straw. That's a promise, or else he won't be writing again anytime soon.

About the Illustrator

MARTIN MATJE

is an illustrato